Cinderella

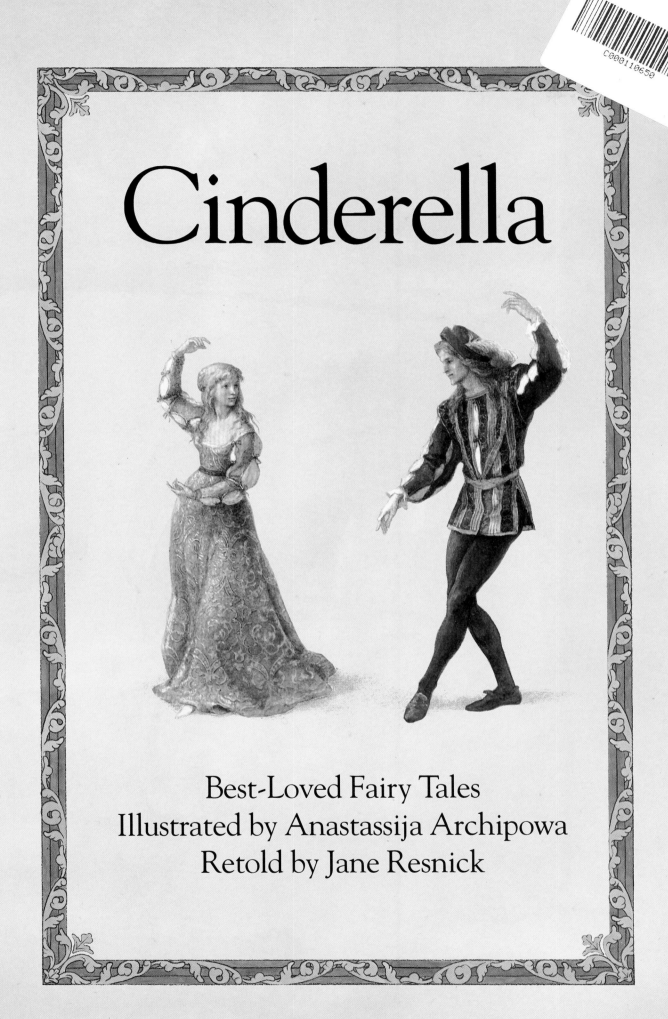

Best-Loved Fairy Tales
Illustrated by Anastassija Archipowa
Retold by Jane Resnick

DERRYDALE BOOKS

New York

Copyright © Verlag J.F. Schreiber GmbH,
"Esslinger im OBV",
Postfach 285, 7300 Esslingen/West Germany
English text © 1990 Joshua Morris Publishing, Inc.
221 Danbury Road, Wilton, Connecticut 06897
All rights reserved.
This 1990 edition published by Derrydale Books,
distributed by Outlet Book Company, Inc.,
a Random House Company,
225 Park Avenue South, New York, New York 10003
Printed in Hong Kong.
ISBN 0-517-051427
8 7 6 5 4 3 2 1

Cinderella

There was once a rich man who lived with his wife and daughter in a great house. His wife became very ill and when she knew she was going to die, she left her young daughter with these tender words:

"Do not be sad, my dear child, for I will always watch over you, and the birds of the forest will protect you."

But the girl cried bitterly. And even after a year, she visited her mother's grave faithfully. While she was there, the birds of the forest comforted her.

She became even sadder when her father married a cold, greedy woman with two daughters who laughed at their stepsister for her gentleness and love for the birds. They wanted her father's wealth and were jealous of her beauty.

Because the father was often away and unaware of his household, the stepmother and stepsisters told him that his daughter had become stubborn and bad, and asked to punish her. At first he did not believe them, but his daughter never defended herself. So from that day on, she was given an old, ugly dress to wear, and she was treated like the lowest of servants.

Her sisters teased her by throwing peas and lentils into the ashes and making her pick them out. In this way, she became covered with cinders— and they called her Cinderella.

Alone and sad, Cinderella had only the birds of the forest to comfort her when she visited her mother's grave each day.

One day, when the father left for a long journey, he asked the stepsisters what gift they would like upon his return.

"A dress of silk, jewels and pearls," they demanded.

"Cinderella?" he asked sadly, for he thought she was as awful as he had been told.

"I would like a branch if one brushes against you," she said.

Her sisters laughed at this.

"Stupid girl!" the older said as soon as the father left. Then she

threw a handful of lentils into the ashes.

"Sort these!" she ordered. "Save the clean ones for soup."

Cinderella fell to her knees and began sorting the lentils.

When the father returned, the two sisters showed off their new finery, but Cinderella took the hazel twig her father brought her and planted it by her mother's grave. In time, it grew into a fine tree, loved by all the birds of the forest.

One day Cinderella scraped her knee on the hearth. When

she went to her mother's grave she wept and said: *Hear my wish, my hazel tree: I need some comfort for my knee.*

A silver bird flew down from the branches. With its own feather, the bird brushed the soot from Cinderella's knee.

When Cinderella got back to the house, she found her step-sisters in a frantic rush.

"Bring me my ribbons! Where are my pearls?" they cried.

"The King has invited the daughters of the house to a ball," the stepmother said. "It will last three nights and the prince will choose a bride."

"Why am I not to go?" Cinderella asked.

"You!" cried the stepmother. "You are too ugly and dirty!"

But the father, while he was preparing to leave for yet another journey, overheard her.

"She *is* my daughter," he said.

"If she can finish her work, she can go," she replied.

But as soon as the father left, the stepmother threw a huge handful of lentils into the ashes.

"If you sort these and bring me a bowl of good ones in an hour, you may go," she said.

Cinderella ran to her mother's grave and said: *Hear my wish, my hazel tree: I need my birds to work for me.*

The little silver bird and all the other forest birds flew to the kitchen. They began picking the lentils from the ashes with their beaks and dropping the good ones into a bowl.

Before the hour, the task was complete and Cinderella took the bowl to her stepmother.

"I have finished," she said in a voice filled with hope.

The stepmother was startled and did not know what to do. She was determined to keep Cinderella from going to the ball, for she knew she was far lovelier than her own daughters.

"You still cannot go," she said. "You are filthy and have no clothes for a ball."

Cinderella wept and wept. Her stepmother became so annoyed that she marched into the kitchen, filled a huge bowl with lentils and threw them all into the ashes.

"You may go if you pick these out in an hour," she said. She was sure Cinderella could not.

So Cinderella ran to her mother's grave again and said: *Hear my wish, my hazel tree: I need my birds to work for me.*

And the silver bird flew down again and within an hour all the lentils were sorted. But this time, her stepmother was very angry and said:

"Go away! I do not believe you did what I ordered. You may not come with us!"

Then she and the stepsisters hurried into the coach that took them to the ball.

Weeping, Cinderella went to her mother's grave once more.

After the silver bird comforted her with his singing, she said: *Hear my wish, my hazel tree: I need a dress to cover me.*

At this, the bird flew down with a magnificent gold and silver dress with beautiful dancing slippers. Cinderella thanked the bird. She bathed and dressed and went to the ball.

There, everyone stared at her, for she was, by far, the most beautiful girl in the room. Even her own stepsisters and stepmother admired her without realizing who she was.

As soon as Cinderella entered the ballroom, the prince asked her to dance. From that moment

he would dance with no one else. Beautiful Cinderella danced in a dream of happiness.

But as the hour grew late, Cinderella knew she must go home, for she was afraid she would be punished if her family knew she had been to the ball.

"I will take you home," said the prince eagerly, but she fled down the stairs so fast that he could not catch her.

Cinderella was in her old dress by the hearth when her stepmother and stepsisters returned. They never suspected that she was the beautiful maiden who stole the prince's heart.

On the second evening of the

ball, her father was still away, so as soon as her stepsisters and stepmother drove off in the coach, Cinderella ran to her mother's grave and said: *Hear my wish, my hazel tree: I need a dress to cover me.*

The bird brought her another dress even more beautiful than the first one, more intricately embroidered and with more gold than silver. The dancing slippers were like the wings of delicate, brightly colored butterflies.

At the ball, once again, everyone marveled at Cinderella's beauty, the prince most of all. He had eyes only for Cinderella and would dance with no one else. The music seemed to be just for the two of them.

"Please let me take you

home," the prince said to his mysterious dancing partner. "I want to know where you live and who your father is."

But when the hour was late, Cinderella escaped, and even though the prince followed closely, she ran swiftly into the woods and climbed a tree. She hid in the tree until he gave up the search.

When her stepsisters arrived home, they found her asleep as before and thought she could not hear their grumbling about the beautiful girl who captured the prince's attention.

"Never mind," they said to one another. "Perhaps she will not be at the ball tomorrow. Or perhaps the prince will notice one of us instead."

On the third night of the ball, Cinderella again waited for her stepmother and stepsisters to leave. She ran to her mother's grave where she said: *Hear my wish, my hazel tree: I need a dress to cover me.*

The bird brought her a magnificent dress that glowed like shimmering sunbeams and slippers that sparkled like dazzling crystal. That night the prince vowed that he would not lose her. During the ball, his servants covered the stairs with sticky pine tar.

When Cinderella felt she must leave, she slipped from his embrace and fled. But this time, the stairs prevented her from running so quickly. One of her slippers stuck in the tar and she had to leave it behind on the stair or be caught.

The next morning the prince took the slipper to his father, the king, and said:

"My bride will be the maiden whose foot fits this slipper. She is the beautiful princess I have danced with every night."

The prince set out that day

and traveled to the house of every person invited to the ball. Hopeful girls all over the kingdom pretended to have lost a slipper, for they were anxious to be queen. But the lovely slipper was too small for everyone who tried it on.

Cinderella's house was the last place the prince came to.

"Surely, I will find my princess here," he thought.

The father was still not at home, so the stepmother took her older daughter into her room to try the slipper on.

"It is too small," the girl said. "Four toes will fit but the fifth

will not squeeze in."

"Just bend the toe under," the determined mother said.

"I can hardly walk!" gasped the girl.

But her mother led her daughter out to the prince.

"Come with me," he said graciously, "for the shoe is indeed on your foot."

The girl managed to walk to the carriage without limping, but the prince felt in his heart that something was not right.

As the prince's coach passed Cinderella's mother's grave, the birds of the forest flew around his coach. The silver bird whispered in the prince's ear: *Good prince, you know not what you do. Her foot is bent inside that shoe!*

So the prince asked the step-sister to get down from the coach and walk with him under the trees. But the girl's toes were so cramped she could barely move.

"You are not my true bride," he said angrily, and returned her

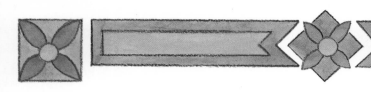

to her parents' house.

"It must be my other daughter whom you want," the stepmother said. She forced her other child to squeeze her foot into the slipper.

Once again the prince was fooled until the little silver bird whispered to him: *Good prince, you know not what you do. Her foot is bent inside that shoe!*

And as he was bringing the girl back to her door, the father returned home.

"Is there no other girl here?" the prince asked.

"None but my two," the stepmother replied.

"But there's Cinderella," the father said.

"She's just a servant girl," the stepmother replied sharply.

At last, Cinderella's father grew angry and said, "She's *my* daughter and she *will* be given a chance!" And he sent for her.

The slipper slid easily onto Cinderella's foot, and this time the prince knew in his heart that he had found the right maiden. So he led her gently to his coach and took her away with him.

As they passed the hazel tree, the silver bird sang:

Good prince, you've found your bride so true: See how her foot fits in the shoe!

Soon the king held another ball—in honor of the wedding of the prince and Cinderella.